"I Don't Want To"

THE STORY OF JONAH

By Marilyn Lashbrook

Illustrated by Stephanie McFetridge Britt

ME TOO!
BOOKS

ROPER PRESS, INC.
DALLAS, TEXAS

The story of Jonah is filled with action. Your child will giggle as you stress the highlighted onomatopoeia (sound suggests meaning) words in the first few readings. Soon, your little one will be able to say the words with you. When you feel your child knows these special words, pause when you come to them and allow him or her to fill in the word. Remember, your child's laughter does not mean he is not taking the lesson to heart. It only means you will be asked to read the story again and again. As God's truth is presented repeatedly, your child's understanding will grow.

Library of Congress Catalog Card Number: 87-60264
ISBN 0-86606-428-1

Art direction and design by
  Chris Schechner Graphic Design

"I Don't Want To"

THE STORY OF JONAH

By Marilyn Lashbrook
Illustrated by Stephanie McFetridge Britt

Taken from the book of Jonah

ME TOO!
BOOKS

God spoke to Jonah.
What did He say?
"Go! Go to preach in Nineveh!"

NINEVEH →

But Jonah was not happy.
"I don't want to!,"
Jonah said to himself,
"and I won't go."

"I will pack my things and run away.
I will go so far
God will never find me."

Jonah hurried to the shore.

He paid for a ride on a big boat.

"God will not find me here," Jonah thought.

But God sees wherever we are.
He hears whatever we think.
God knew where Jonah was.

And God sent a storm to tell him so.

The wind went *whish*!
The waves went *swish*!
And the big boat was tossed to and fro.

Zing went Jonah right out of the boat.
Splash went Jonah right into the sea.

Glub ... glub ... glub went Jonah
as he sank slowly to the bottom.

But God did not want Jonah to drown.

So God sent a great *BIG* fish . . .

. . . to swallow Jonah!

Slippery, *slimy*.
Jonah slid to the fish's belly.
Ishy, *squishy*.
What a place to be!

It was dark inside the fish.
It was hot inside the fish.
It was stinky inside the fish.
Phewy!

Whoosh, *swoosh* went the fish's stomach.
Thump, *thump* went Jonah's heart.
It was time to pray!
Now, Jonah wanted to obey.

God heard Jonah's prayer.

He sent the fish to shore.

Zing went Jonah right out of the fish.
Splat went Jonah right onto the beach.

"Moan, moan, groan," went Jonah as he picked himself up from the ground.

God spoke to Jonah.
What did He say?
"Go! Go to preach in Nineveh."

And what do you think
Jonah did this time?

He headed for Nineveh in a hurry!

Jonah had learned to quickly obey.

ME TOO!
B O O K S

For Ages 2-5

SOMEONE TO LOVE
THE STORY OF CREATION

TWO BY TWO
THE STORY OF NOAH'S FAITH

"I DON'T WANT TO"
THE STORY OF JONAH

"I MAY BE LITTLE"
THE STORY OF DAVID'S GROWTH

"I'LL PRAY ANYWAY"
THE STORY OF DANIEL

WHO NEEDS A BOAT?
THE STORY OF MOSES

"GET LOST LITTLE BROTHER"
THE STORY OF JOSEPH

THE WALL THAT DID NOT FALL
THE STORY OF RAHAB'S FAITH

NO TREE FOR CHRISTMAS
THE STORY OF JESUS' BIRTH

"NOW I SEE"
THE STORY OF THE MAN BORN BLIND

DON'T ROCK THE BOAT!
THE STORY OF THE MIRACULOUS CATCH

OUT ON A LIMB
THE STORY OF ZACCHAEUS

ME TOO!
R E A D E R S

For Ages 5-8

IT'S NOT MY FAULT
MAN'S BIG MISTAKE

GOD, PLEASE SEND FIRE!
ELIJAH AND THE PROPHETS OF BAAL

TOO BAD, AHAB!
NABOTH'S VINEYARD

THE WEAK STRONGMAN
SAMSON

NOTHING TO FEAR
JESUS WALKS ON WATER

THE BEST DAY EVER
THE STORY OF JESUS

THE GREAT SHAKE-UP
MIRACLES IN PHILIPPI

TWO LADS AND A DAD
THE PRODIGAL SON

Available at your local
bookstore
or from
Roper Press
4737-A Gretna
Dallas, Texas 75207
1-800-284-0158